THE SECRETS OF

CRICKET KARLSSON

Kristina Sigunsdotter
Illustrated by Ester Eriksson

Translated by Julia Marshall

Hi

THiS BooK BELONGS To
CRiCKET KARLSSON.
SNEAK-READ AT YOUR OWN RiSK.

1

My name is Cricket Karlsson, I'm eleven years old and I'm in Class 5C. My best friend is Noa. She's in 5B. My life is pretty good, except I just got chicken pox.

FORGET what I just wrote! From this moment the following applies: My name is Cricket Karlsson, I'm eleven years old and my life is a CATASTROPHE. I got ONE HUNDRED AND THREE chicken poxes and had to stay home from school for TWO weeks. When I got back, my best friend Noa had gone off with the horse girls. Now she pretends I don't exist. I hate school and I hate my life.

On Friday in art class we had to draw self-portraits. At first I was going to draw the 103 chicken poxes, but I drew myself as a mole instead. I've heard it's a very lonely animal. Our art teacher Pikka said I'd drawn myself wrong, that you don't do self-portraits like that. So I had to draw another one.

ONE KIND OF SELF-PORTRAIT

ANOTHER KIND OF SELF-PORTRAIT

2

The family came for Sunday lunch. Grandpa, his girlfriend
Bobbie, and Aunt Frannie. As usual they only talked about
boring things. Why do grown-ups talk so much about
things they don't even like? Like illnesses and life crises
and the end of the world.

Aunt Frannie was quiet. She often is over Sunday lunch.
We usually make secret signs to each other when the
others are extra boring, but this time she just stared at the
table. Aunt Frannie is an artist, like I will be when I'm an
adult. She started drawing on her table napkin: a horse
with wild eyes and a girl with long legs.

Suddenly, right in the middle of some distant relative's
marriage crisis, she screamed out loud. Then she threw
her wine glass at the wall. It made a big red stain. They
couldn't get rid of it, so Dad put a picture over it. Which

is a shame because the stain was pretty, like one of those old trees with crannies where you can hide secret things.

When everyone had gone, I asked why Aunt Frannie had screamed. Dad said it was nothing to worry about. She just wanted attention. My mother sighed. That's my hate-sound, when she sighs. Every morning when we sit at the breakfast table, she looks at me first, then at Dad and then she sighs. She's done that as long as I can remember. She also sighs if we're having people to visit. Especially if Aunt Frannie is coming. Then it's an extra-sighy sigh.

I don't understand what Ma has against Aunt Frannie; I like her a lot. When I was little, she used to babysit me all the time. We always did art. Once we found a can of black paint in the garage and we made an installation in our garden. We painted all the pots and the magnolia tree black. *A thousand years of black*, we called it. My parents were so angry they didn't speak to me for a whole evening. Aunt Frannie wasn't allowed to babysit me again after that.

A THOUSAND YEARS OF BLACK ➡

3

Today we had phys ed. We have it almost constantly because our teacher Ann-Louise loves phys ed. Her eyes shine when she climbs the wall bars so she can shout out orders about where to put everything.

"The barre goes there, the beam here, trapeze here, box over there!" Once she got so overexcited her face turned purple. She had to climb down and sit with her head between her knees so she didn't faint.

I hate phys ed. Most of all I hate it when everyone, including Ann-Louise, stands and watches to see if you'll fall off the equipment. Mitten and I refused to do gym so we had to play table tennis instead. Mitten smelled of sweat.

My mood improved slightly when we had pancakes for lunch. I love them. Ideally, they come with apple sauce, but at school we get lingonberry jam and that's okay too.

GOLDILOCKS

I stood behind Goldilocks (5A) in the lunch queue.
His jacket smelled of diesel. That's because he gets a ride to
school on a moped with his cool big brother. When I turn
fifteen, I'm getting a moped, lime green with a top box.

When we sat in the dining room, I saw the horse girls
through the window. They were galloping across the
schoolyard, neighing. Noa wasn't with them, and I think
I know why. She's ashamed of the birthmark on her thigh,
just below her butt.

This evening Grandpa and Bobbie popped in. Grandpa said Aunt Frannie is in the hospital, something called Adult Psych. I saw Dad rolling his eyes at my mother. When I wanted to know what disease Aunt Frannie had, Dad said an imaginary disease, and everyone laughed, not because it was funny. I asked if we could visit her at the hospital and Dad said we'll see.

4

This morning I rang Adult Psychiatric Ward 84 and asked if I could visit Aunt Frannie. The woman who answered sounded pleased and said absolutely, as long as I didn't take anything with me that Aunt Frannie could hurt herself with. I hadn't thought I would. I'll take her a packet of vape pods. Aunt Frannie loves them.

I have to buy them at the kiosk down by the pond where the man doesn't ask for ID. There are always kids from high school standing outside smoking. Sometimes Goldilocks is there with his cool brother. I'll never smoke. The pictures on the packets are horrible. Sometimes you don't know if it's a rotten ear or a shrivelled foot. Also, Aunt Frannie reckons you get a hairy tongue if you smoke.

She's said she'll stop smoking after summer but till then she'll smoke like a brush-maker. I like that word. Our class teacher Rock said that brush-making was a job blind people did in the olden days. Bobbie says that Grandpa swears like a brush-maker.

In the clearing up behind our house Noa and I pretend to be blind brush-makers. We sit on rocks and close our eyes and make brushes out of pine needles and fir cones. We swear the worst swear words we can think of. But not anymore, of course...

When I think about the fun Noa and I used to have my chest hurts as if my heart is an overcooked potato about to become mash.

THINGS NOA IS GOOD AT:

- MAKING SCULPTURES
- LAUGHING SO ALL HER TEETH SHOW
- PLAYING THE DRUMS
- SEWING
- BEING FUNNY
- KEEPING SECRETS
- THREADING WORMS ON FISHHOOKS WITHOUT SQUEAMING
- BIKING WITH NO HANDS
- TELLING GHOST STORIES
- SQUEEZING BLACKHEADS WITHOUT LEAVING A MARK
- MAKING TOASTIES
- CUTTING HAIR
- BEING SERIOUS AT THE RIGHT MOMENT

5

I had the wolf hour last night. Aunt Frannie taught me
that the wolf hour is when you wake in the middle of the
night and can't get back to sleep. And everything feels
wrong and sad but you don't know why. Aunt Frannie
says that going for a walk can help. If I go out in the wolf
hour, I sometimes do bad things. It's as if the darkness
makes me. I do things that would make my mother sigh
her longest extra-sighy sigh, like kicking the streetlight
till it goes out or filling water balloons with jelly and
chucking them off the overbridge. But last night I just lay
in bed and stared at the ceiling.

6

School is as horrible as ever. Noa avoided me the whole
day. At least I think so, because I avoided everyone.
At break times, I locked myself in the bathroom so no
one had to see my sorry face.

When I got home, my mother was cleaning the attic and asked me to help her. We burned everything we weren't going to save or give to the City Mission in the garden incinerator. It was so much fun I even forgot about Noa. The most fun was clearing out the cupboard Ma used when she was studying economics. She lived in a student hostel that always smelled of fish because one boy used to cook fish fingers in the toaster. She hasn't been able to eat toast since then without throwing up.

In the cupboard I found a shoebox full of old postcards from a boy called "Matt in Madras." My mother must have met him when she went to India. One postcard had

a photo stuck to it. Matt in Madras was lying with his head in my mother's lap. He had long curly hair and gold earrings. She looked young and her eyes were shining.

When I asked who Matt in Madras might be, she went bright red. Then she was cross because I'd rummaged in her things, and she locked the cupboard and said that was enough for today.

Clearing out stuff is the job my mother loves best in the world. When she does it, she has almost the same glitter in her eyes as when Matt in Madras was lying in her lap. For her next birthday I'm going to give her a box of clutter to sort through.

The worst thing is if she cleans out my room when I'm not home. She always throws out precious things, like the sculpture called *Self-portrait of two lost souls* that Noa and I made from chewing gum. It took several weeks to make, plus Noa got inflammation of the jaw, all for nothing.

I haven't dared tell Noa that Ma threw it away. Not that she'd care anymore.

I miss her!!! The only person who wants to be with me at school is Mitten, but he's so boring, he makes dead people fall asleep. Besides that, he's afraid of EVERYTHING

THINGS MITTEN IS AFRAID OF:

- CATS, DOGS AND BIRDS
- THE FIELD BEHIND SCHOOL
- TOENAIL CLIPPINGS
- DOOR HANDLES
- THE CHANGING ROOMS
- JUMPING THE BOX
- GOING ON THE BEAM
- BALL SPORTS
- LIVER PASTE
- GROWNUPS (EXCEPT HIS MOTHER AND THE LUNCH LADIES)
- STOVE ELEMENTS
- INSECTS
- PLASTIC GLOVES
- GIFT RIBBON

7

The horse girls look at me and whisper when I walk past.
I wonder what they're saying. Best case, they're only
pretending to say something, to upset me, to show they
have POWER. Worst case, they KNOW things.

Noa and I swore on our dead grandmothers and her
father who left that we'll take each other's secrets to the
GRAVE, but now I don't know if I can trust her on that.
It wasn't even THINKABLE then that she'd abandon me.
Now that she has, anything could happen.

SECRETS i HAVE
ONLY TOLD NOA:

★ I STOLE A PACK OF TAMPONS (THOUGH
   i HAVEN'T EVEN GOT MY PERIOD YET)

★ ONLY MY RIGHT BREAST HAS STARTED
   GROWING

★ iT WAS ME WHO GRAFFiTiED THE STONE
   BEHiND THE SCHOOL (i WROTE THE NAME
   OF A ROCK BAND i DON'T LiKE SO NO ONE
   WOULD SUSPECT ME)

★ I TOOK TWENTY DOLLARS FROM THE SEWiNG
   TEACHER AND HiD iT iN MY DESK

★ I CUT A HOLE iN MY BACKPACK SO i
   COULD GET A NEW ONE

★ i'VE SET FiRE TO GRASS iN THE FOREST

★ ONCE i DRANK BOBBiE'S CHERRY LiQUEUR

★ I SOMETiMES SHOVE A SOCK iN MY PANTS
   AND PRETEND i'M A BOY

THINGS I HAVEN'T
EVEN TOLD NOA:

- I'M JEALOUS OF HER BECAUSE
SHE'S GOT HER PERIOD

- SOMETIMES I'M SCARED THAT
MA AND DAD WILL DIE

- ONCE WHEN WE HAD SCHOOL
ORIENTEERING I URGENTLY NEEDED
TO POOP AND I DID IT IN THE FOREST

8

The horse girls have made their own tattoos, the Chinese character for horse. They've done them for real, with needles and ink from an old pen. Noa too. Her mother will be mad as a rattlesnake when she sees it.

I've borrowed a book about psychiatric hospitals from the school library. It says that in the olden days they called them lunatic asylums and the patients got spun in a special machine to calm them down.

In the olden days, horse girls who tattooed themselves and galloped around in their short shorts were probably locked up in the lunatic asylum.

Today after school I visited Aunt Frannie. I had to ring a bell to be let in. It smelled strange inside, and the walls

were painted a cacky yellow. Aunt Frannie thought we could sit on the balcony for a bit. She was pleased about the vape pods. I got to click them in for her, then I told her about Noa and the horse girls. Aunt Frannie said she loves horses but she's scared of horse girls. Then we talked about horses for almost an hour.

Aunt Frannie's biggest dream is to ride a horse along a beach in the moonlight.

I told her I'd had the wolf hour and Aunt Frannie told me she has it all the time now. That's why she's locked in the psych ward.

Then an old lady came along who thought I was her mother, and she smoked an actual cigarette till she turned yellow. When it was finished she flapped her hands and said: "Crap, crap."

The lady has Tourette's syndrome. That's an illness when you make sounds and movements without wanting to.

PSYCHIATRIC ILLNESSES i DON'T WANT:

• MICROPSIA / MACROPSIA: YOU THINK PARTS OF YOUR BODY ARE SHRINKING OR GROWING
• ALIEN HAND SYNDROME : YOUR HAND DOES THINGS ALL BY ITSELF

• COTARD'S SYNDROME: YOU'RE CONVINCED YOU'RE DEAD AND ROTTING AWAY

• HOARDING SICKNESS: YOU CAN'T THROW ANYTHING AWAY AND YOU SAVE EVERYTHING, FOR EXAMPLE JUNK AND LEFTOVERS

• STENDHALS SYNDROME: YOU GET DIZZY, HAVE HEART PALPITATIONS, FAINT OR HALLUCINATE WHEN YOU LOOK AT ART

31

9

Today we had group activity. We had to paint a picture of the future. I was Last One Standing when everyone was picked, so our art teacher Pikka decided I would go with Anna H, Anna P and flaky Josephine (also known as the Dweebs). They hated all my suggestions but had no ideas of their own, so in the end Pikka said we should paint ourselves as old people. It turned out all right. Flaky Josephine helped me with the wrinkles. Too bad she talks so quietly, otherwise we could be friends. I'd have to get a hearing aid, or I suppose we could learn sign language.

Mitten sat beside me at lunch. He's started giving me presents. Today it was a back scratcher. He said they're good because you don't have to use your nails. Mitten is scared of nails.

Then we went to the library to read about more mental illnesses. Marianne the librarian sat hidden behind a huge pile of books as usual. Only her curly hair showed. Marianne speaks almost as softly as flaky Josephine, so I never know what she's saying. There is a story going around that Marianne peed on the floor in the library, for reasons unknown.

While we sat reading, the horse girls came in. They whinnied and shrieked that they wanted books about horses. Marianne went completely red in the face. When I saw Noa my heart missed a beat. When she saw I was there, she left. I seem to be about as attractive as a bag of dog poop.

Next week our whole year group is going on a school trip. I wonder how that will be. No doubt Mitten will want to sit next to me on the bus. Hope he brings deodorant.

Dad has to work, so just Ma and I are having Fun Friday. In a normal family, Fun Friday would be something to look forward to, but my mother has decided that the whole family is going on a diet, and not just any old diet, but the STONE AGE DIET. Apparently, it's incredibly healthy and good for you. Ma has a cookbook—*Roots & Nuts: Cooking like a Stone Ager*—that she is slavishly following. It might be okay if she actually followed the recipes, but she's too impatient.

According to my mother, Fun Friday in the Stone Age means rock-hard taco shells made from burned cauliflower dough, filled with a mess of uncertain substances. No cheese. I understand why the Stone Agers decided to stop being Stone Agers and became normal people.

Our class supervisor Rock told us that when there was famine in Sweden people baked bread out of bark. It was probably on a par with Ma's taco shells. Rock probably would have loved living in the Stone Age when everything was made from rocks. She collects stones, that's why she's called Rock. Once she brought her whole collection to school, and it was just a box full of ordinary stones. I feel a little sad thinking about Rock and her stones.

Luckily, I get food at school too. If you follow two important rules, school food is pretty good.

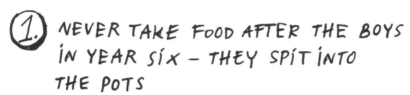

1. NEVER TAKE FOOD AFTER THE BOYS IN YEAR SIX – THEY SPIT INTO THE POTS

2. NEVER LEAVE YOUR FOOD UNATTENDED

Noa and I normally watched each other's trays if one of us had to go and get something. But that didn't work either because we couldn't help, say, putting a potato in the other one's glass of milk while they were away.

Before Aunt Frannie ended up in the hospital, I used to bike home to her place to eat modern-day food. Aunt Frannie loves cheese. All her meals include some form of it. We experiment with different cheese dishes. One of our best is cheese-on-cheese-in-cheese, which is cheese doodles dipped in cheese dip, wrapped in cheese slices.

Once Aunt Frannie and I made soup out of sweets. It was coal-black and possibly the most revolting thing ever made. Or maybe the troll stew Noa and I made when we were small was slightly more disgusting. We filled a pot with everything we could find in the kitchen and put it out in the playhouse till it went rotten. We peed in it too.

I wonder if Aunt Frannie gets cheese at Adult Psychiatric Ward 84.

I've been to visit Aunt Frannie again. I go in secret.
Ma and Dad probably wouldn't like me being there.
I wonder if Dad is ashamed of having a little sister in the
adult psychiatric ward. I'd never be ashamed of my little
sister! Whatever she did.

I gave Aunt Frannie a drawing of a horse in the moonlight. She said I'm good at drawing, and that I should do
art. Aunt Frannie looks really tired. She says it's because
of the drugs, which make her fuzzy. When I asked if I
should bring cheese-on-cheese-in-cheese next time, she
said she doesn't feel like eating anything at all.

Aunt Frannie has a lot of marks on her arms. Like in a
prison cell, where the prisoner draws a mark on the wall
every day to get through it. When I told her that, she got
tears in her eyes. She said the psychiatric ward feels like

a prison, or a ZOO with a lot of strange animals locked up together. If Aunt Frannie were a strange animal, she'd probably be a strange tiger.

By the way, I suspect Dad knows I visit Aunt Frannie because this morning he gave me money to buy a treat and said: "Don't tell your mother."

12

I only have scabs left now after the chicken pox. Some are
on my hands. I've tried to hide them, but today at lunch
one of the horse girls shrieked that I was disgusting. Noa
just stared at her tray as if she'd never seen a tray before.

At lunch break two of the horse girls had an argument.
They pulled each other's hair until there were big tufts on
the floor. A teacher went past but he pretended not to see.
He might be afraid of the horse girls too.

Mitten wants to go out with me. He wrote it on a piece
of paper. I haven't answered because I don't want him to
be sad, so now I have to avoid him.

Today when I got to Adult Psychiatric Ward 84 Dad was there. He and Aunt Frannie were drinking coffee on the balcony. Dad thought the coffee tasted like fox pee. He looked sad, but when we went home, he was happy. He said I was clever to have visited Aunt Frannie. That it was probably helping her get better. Then he gave me money again.

13

Last night I crept up to the attic with a torch. It was really easy to pick open the cupboard with a hairpin. I found a box inside that I couldn't open, as well as more clues about Matt in Madras. Including a love letter saying he wanted Ma to go with him on a round-the-world trip.

That's probably the last thing Dad would suggest. Dad's afraid of flying and so we never even go to the Mediterranean, which my mother suggests every summer. We always end up going to Grandpa and Bobbie's holiday house outside Gnesta. There's a cottage we can stay in, and Dad can hunt wild boars at night. What he doesn't know is that I go through the forest in the daytime yelling out and peeing in the bushes to scare them away.

Ma likes the sea better than the forest. She's scared of wild pigs and all the creepy-crawlies that live in the trees.

Grandpa told me that if you stand with your legs wide apart, when a wild pig comes, it can run between your legs and slice you up the middle with one of its stiletto-sharp tusks. THWACK! Just like that, you're cut in half and dead. Grandpa loves talking about things you can die of. "Worst case, you'll fall off and die!" he calls if you're up a ladder, for example. That's maybe why Aunt Frannie has "a problem with her nerves," as Bobbie says, because since she was little her father has peppered her with death-dangers.

💀 THINGS GRANDPA SAYS YOU CAN DIE FROM:

- 💀 WALKING BEHIND A TRACTOR WHICH SUDDENLY GOES INTO REVERSE AND SQUASHES YOU
- 💀 SINKING INTO A MUDDY DITCH AND RUNNING OUT OF AIR
- 💀 DOING THINGS WITH CABLES
- 💀 SWIMMING AFTER YOU'VE EATEN
- 💀 GETTING LOST IN THE FOREST
- 💀 FALLING FROM A LADDER
- 💀 DIVING ONTO AN IRON SPIKE
- 💀 GETTING A CHICKEN BONE IN YOUR THROAT
- 💀 MEETING AN ANGRY MOTHER MOOSE IN THE FOREST
- 💀 FALLING DOWNSTAIRS
- 💀 FALLING FROM A CLIMBING WALL
- 💀 EATING RED BERRIES FROM BUSHES
- 💀 EATING MUSHROOMS THAT AREN'T CHANTERELLES OR BOLETES
- 💀 EATING MUSHROOMS THAT LOOK LIKE CHANTERELLES

I didn't use to care where we went for holidays, as long as Noa came too. We became best friends our first year at school and we've spent every summer together since then. First, four weeks at Grandpa and Bobbie's, then four weeks camping with her mother. That way we don't end up on our own (Noa is also an only child) and our parents get time out.

I wonder what my parents do when they have time out. Probably they sort through important papers because they say they never have time for that when I'm with them. Maybe they do love stuff as well. My mother usually sighs and looks at Dad and says: "I wonder why I fell in love with you." Then Dad usually gives her a kiss and my stomach fizzes like a soda drink.

I suspect they do more than kiss because I EXIST. But when I think about that I get an urgent need to pour dishwashing liquid in my ears and rinse out my brain.

14

Today I met Noa in the corridor. She immediately started looking at her phone. She was wearing new chalk-white jeans just like the ones the horse girls wear.

When I reached my locker it was as if I'd turned into an aquarium full of tears. I had to rush into the bathroom and empty out a bit. I looked in the mirror while I cried, and I looked like a really good actor. Maybe I should be a film star. I wonder if you can be a film star and a famous artist at the same time?

It's been decided that we're going to Grandpa and Bobbie's again this summer. My parents are expecting I'll spend the rest of the summer with Noa and her mother. I can't tell them the truth.

I wonder if the horse girls understand how fantastic and cool Noa is.

She doesn't look as happy anymore. Last summer we scratched a mosquito bite each and mixed blood and became blood sisters. Then we wrote a contract in mosquito blood that we'd always be best friends, and we chanted a magic rhyme.

This Spell is true
with paper and blood
we're bound, me and
you. BF's to the end of
time and space remote
where Stars are purple
and God is a goat.

When I think of that contract it feels as if my heart is crushed to mashed potato. Strange how everything can change just because you're sick for two weeks. Maybe everything will go back to normal if I get chicken pox again? Except my mother says you can only get it once in a lifetime.

I went to Adult Psychiatric Ward 84 after school, but Aunt Frannie wasn't there. I drank fox pee coffee with the Smoking Woman instead. I told her about Noa and the horse girls and cried a little. The Smoking Woman flapped her arms and said: "Crap, crap."

Aunt Frannie was allowed to go home to her apartment!
I went there after school. But first I bought two green
cakes from the bakery.

I asked Aunt Frannie if she was better now, and she said
she'd lied to the doctor that she was so she could come
home. She said being in the hospital made her feel more
depressed.

She didn't eat any cake and she wanted to go to bed
even though it was only five o'clock. She said I could stay
and paint if I wanted to, so I stayed for a bit. Then I ate
the other cake as well and got stomachache.

When I came home, I started a new chewing gum
project, but it wasn't as much fun without Noa. Plus,
I only had ten pieces of chewing gum, so it was just a
small lump. *The pink poop's last sigh*, I called it.

16

School days are incredibly long when you spend every break sitting in the bathroom. Even though I can draw while I'm there, time passes unbelievably slowly. Mitten gives me mournful looks in every class.

On my way home, I saw Noa. She was guarding the horse girls' bags while they were galloping over the schoolyard. I hid behind Rock's car, then biked after them to the stables. I found a really good pine tree that I could climb up and spy from.

The horse girls all changed into jodhpurs and took their horses out into the sun. They groomed them and laughed and blew bubblegum balloons. Noa carried hay bales and sprayed the horse girls' riding boots with a hose. I thought she looked like a slave.

Then Noa said something funny that made the horse girls laugh. I got such a pain in my heart I had to clutch a pinecone hard to make my hand hurt so I could forget my heart for a moment.

Then they rode off. Noa was riding a white horse with a strange tail.

The horse girls had hung their white jeans over a plank and I couldn't help throwing mud pies at them before I biked home.

Dad was home and asked if I wanted to go with him to see Aunt Frannie, and of course I did. He'd made lasagne. When we got there, Dad had to call, "I know you're home!" into the letter slot so Aunt Frannie would open the door. She said she'd been asleep and it was probably true because her cheek was really wrinkly.

It always smells good at Aunt Frannie's. Paint and smoke. Even though she doesn't smoke anymore.

Aunt Frannie only ate a bite of Dad's lasagne. Then she said she couldn't paint anymore. Everything felt so sad I cried in the car on the way home. I took the opportunity to cry a little about Noa as well.

I wish I'd never got chicken pox and that Mitten would stop being in love with me and that I'd get a little sister and that Aunt Frannie would start painting again.

17

Someone told the horse girls that I sit in the bathroom at break times so they've started calling me Crapula. I suspect it was Anna P who told because I think she's in love with Mitten. By the way, he's given me another present but I haven't opened it yet.

The horse girls yelled out in the corridor that I wear ugly clothes. They're not the only ones who think so. My mother says I have terrible fashion sense. Her biggest dream is for me to go clothes shopping with her at the mall. I'd rather eat cat food.

On the other hand, if Noa came too... We could pretend to be interested and go around feeling the clothes and exclaiming, "Oh, what a GORGEOUS scarf! Such fantastic QUALITY!"

I have two role models: Aunt Frannie and Gargamel from *The Smurfs*. All the clothes I wear are from going to second-hand shops with Noa. Noa sews her own clothes, or at least she did before she started going around with the horse girls. Now she wears the exact same clothes they do. Super-white jeans, cropped T-shirts and riding boots.

I tried to sew a pair of trousers once in sewing class, but one leg was too thin, so I looked like half a sausage. I'm worst in class at sewing. Our teacher Dana says it's because I have no patience, but that's not true. I have plenty of patience, just not for boring things like PINNING and HEMMING.

THINGS i HAVE PATIENCE FOR:

❀ DRAWING

❀ TALKING TO NOA ON THE PHONE

❀ PITTING CHERRIES FOR BOBBIE'S CHERRY LIQUEUR

❀ PEELING PRAWNS

❀ MAKING ART

❀ PICKING LINGONBERRIES

❀ SORTING SOCKS

I had the wolf hour again last night. I thought about Noa and went out. Didn't find any water balloons so I threw cucumbers from the bridge instead.

18

We've just finished doing puberty in biology and now we've started on human organs. Rock had a bag of cows' eyes for us to dissect.

We had floury plastic gloves and a scalpel each. Cutting into an eye was really fun. The retina looked like a miniature universe. Mitten turned white and had to go and lie on the couch in the staffroom.

Then I went to Aunt Frannie's. My mother says Aunt Frannie is a bad influence on me because she doesn't have a "proper" job and she smokes. But she doesn't anymore! Fortunately, Dad has persuaded her that I should go there as much as I want. It means he doesn't have to go. Grandpa and Bobbie have gone to Spain.

I read that physical activity and daylight are good for mental health, so I asked Aunt Frannie if she wanted to come out in the sun and eat ice cream, but she didn't want to. She doesn't seem to like the sun anymore. All the blinds are down, so it's like visiting a vampire.

She asked how things were with Noa. I started crying and Aunt Frannie held my hand. Then she got out a packet of brand-new felt pens, the expensive kind I'm saving up for. She said it can be good to draw when you're sad. But when I asked why she'd stopped drawing she didn't answer.

I showed her the chewing gum poop, and she asked if she could keep it and of course she could. She put it on the windowsill beside a wilted fern. It looked really nice.

We ate chips for lunch and watched a movie and Aunt Frannie fell asleep on the sofa. She's really pretty when she sleeps, like someone in a movie about a sleeping person.

I stayed a while and did her enormous pile of dishes.

When I came home Ma ran me a bubble bath. Then she sat on the toilet and read gossip magazines while I lay there. She made more bubbles when the old ones ran out, just like when I was little. It felt so nice I almost told her about Noa, but I was just about to open my mouth when she said:

"Can you ask Noa which weeks you'll be going camping this summer?"

And then my stomach hurt so much I couldn't speak at all. I just made a strange sound that she translated as "yes."

19

Today the doorbell rang and for half a minute I thought it was Noa, till I heard Mitten's voice. Unfortunately, my mother managed to let him in before I had time to fake an infectious illness.

Mitten brought a packet of bath bombs, and he turned bright red when he gave them to me. Luckily, he didn't say anything about the shall-we-go-out note, and I kept thinking up things to do so he wouldn't ask. We made things with clay, drew with my new glitter glue and made green candy floss in the candy floss machine Aunt Frannie gave me for Christmas.

Mitten laughs at everything I say. He says practically nothing. I've never heard anyone laugh like Mitten. It took me a while to realize it was a laugh. It sounds more like an

attack of coughing. Maybe he has a problem with dry air or is hypersensitive to dust, or even to life.

When we'd eaten the candy floss Mitten got an allergic reaction and his mother had to come and get him.

PRESENTS I'VE HAD FROM MITTEN:

* BACK SCRATCHER
* PUZZLE (1000 PIECES)
* OVEN MITTS HE MADE IN SEWING
* SLIPPERS YOU WARM IN THE MICROWAVE
* STRAWBERRY-SCENTED BATH BOMBS

20

I've stopped hiding in the bathroom at breaks but the horse girls still call me Crapula. Even one of the Dweebs said it today when I went past in the corridor. (Wouldn't know if flaky Josephine said it because you can't hear her.)

I try not to care, but the worst thing is that Noa still says nothing at all. She just stares at the ground as if there's something incredibly interesting down there. That's what I can't bear.

I feel like a space alien. I wonder if anyone could be lonelier than me. No one talks to me (except Mitten and I'd rather he didn't). Dad just works. Ma sighs and Aunt Frannie doesn't answer when I phone. I have no friends and still no little sister.

21

THREE THINGS HAVE HAPPENED

1. SOMEONE DREW A POOP ON MY DESK.

2. WE HAD A SURPRISE TEST.

3. I FAKED A STOMACH ULCER.

Our whole year group had a test in Room 1 and Noa sat a few seats in front of me. I'm usually good at statistics but it was impossible to concentrate. All the tables and diagrams looked like mountains and ugly apartment blocks. I said I had an acute stomach ulcer and got to sit in the staffroom till my mother could come and get me.

Today I pretended to be sick because I can't be bothered with school. Tomorrow is the school trip. If it wasn't for that, I'd stay sick for the rest of term, but we're going to a farm to look at the animals and I don't want to miss out.

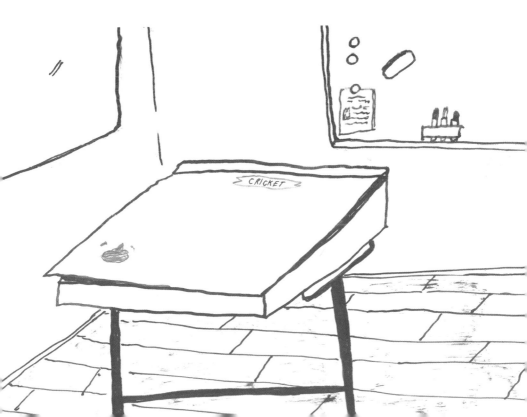

22

DIAGRAM OF MY

CATASTROPHIC LIFE

BORN

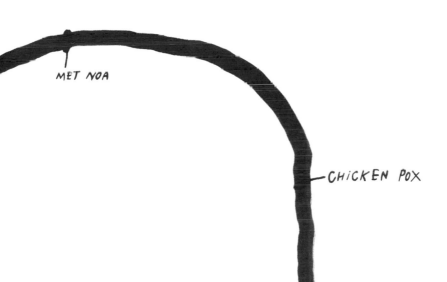

MET NOA

CHICKEN POX

NOA LEFT ME

23

Now we're on our school trip. We're staying near a farm and we'll sleep on the floor in a hall that smells of sweaty feet. I've brought a blow-up mattress and my blue sleeping bag with stars on it. Of course, Mitten has taken the place next to me.

On the way here, Noa sat at the back of the bus beside Goldilocks. He seems interested in her because he laughs at everything she says, so now I hate him a bit. I sat next to flaky Josephine. She taught me how to make friendship bracelets and her dandruff drifted down like snow onto my leg. When we got off the bus Anna H and Anna P appeared and took her away with them.

First we had to go on a quiz walk. Mitten felt sick and got to stay and rest so no one chose me as quiz walk partner. I went with Rock instead. I guess she wanted to be kind because she told me all the answers to the questions. It was actually fun going with Rock because she knows lots of fun facts about animals, such as that chickens are the closest living relatives of T. rexes.

Rock asked me why Noa and I aren't speaking to each other anymore and I couldn't reply because I would have flooded with tears and broken my potato heart in pieces. So I just said: "No idea," and that was the end of that.

We grilled sausages and Rock told ghost stories about a dead grandmother whose liver lay outside her stomach. Mitten was feeling better and tried to hold my hand. His was wet with sweat.

Imagine if Mitten and Goldilocks could fall in love instead. Then they'd leave Noa and me in peace.

I've never been in love, or maybe sometimes with Noa. Like last summer when we went camping, and she happened to sit on a strawberry. She walked around pretending it was a period stain. All the boys went bright red.

It's so snug in the van when we go camping. Noa and I always sleep in the bunk at the back. I especially like the rainbow of plastic strips that hang in the doorway to stop flies. We usually stay on the beach the whole day. Noa always gets lots of freckles, I mostly go red. We build sand sculptures and collect seaweed to use as hair. Once we saw a boy lying on the beach with his willy sticking straight up under the towel. It looked like a tent for mini squirrels. I'm glad I don't have a willy.

The evenings are best of all. Noa's mother usually goes to the pub to find someone to fall in love with and we stay at the campsite drinking juice and playing cards and telling our innermost secrets.

Tomorrow it's time for our farm visit, then it's a dance in the evening. I've brought my best dancing shoes with the flashing soles. I wonder why, really. I'll probably have to dance on my own or, worst case, with Mitten or Rock.

24

A miracle has happened!!!!!!!!!!! This is a historic day!
I can hardly write because my hand is shaking so much.
First, I had two lucky things happen.

1. When we arrived at the farm Mitten refused to leave
    the bus because he was convinced he'd get mad cow
    disease.
2. Goldilocks tried to impress Noa by touching an
    electric fence. But it had so many volts, it threw him
    backwards and his beautiful face turned super-white
    and he had to go back to the bus and rest.

So when it was time to form pairs for the day's activities,
Noa and I were both left over and Rock said: "Noa and
Cricket, today you'll be together!"

You can guess that sent a volt through my heart!

We were given a page with animal questions to answer on our way around the farm. At first, we were completely silent. I didn't know what to say. Then we came to the pigsty and a sow had given birth to small piglets exactly at that moment. The farmer asked if we'd like to hold one each. We sat in the straw with them and mine was white with black spots and so sweet I never wanted to let it go. Noa's piglet was all black. Suddenly Noa looked at me with big, sad eyes and said:

"Do you hate me, Cricket?"

"No," I said, and we hugged, and my neck was completely soaked by her tears.

Then the black piglet pooped on Noa's dress and I said it was a Crapula and she looked happy again.

Noa said she didn't want to be with the horse girls anymore, that she couldn't stand it any longer and that she missed me so badly she was dying. "The horse girls are like a cult," she said. "I got brainwashed. Will you forgive me, Cricket?" I did of course and Noa promised never to leave me again and we hugged again and cried a little more.

I told Noa everything that's happened and that Aunt Frannie has stopped making art. Noa understood straight away how serious this is and said we must do something before it's too late.

On the hillside, we found a completely round stone that we gave to Rock. She was so happy she had tears in her eyes.

In the evening we had the disco. Louise and Eva kissed for ages on the dance floor. Mitten almost choked on a bit of popcorn. Noa and I danced only with each other.

P.S. Now all the scabs from the chicken pox have fallen off = I'm no longer disgusting. There are some small scars left, but you can only see them up close.

25

NOA SLEPT OVER AT MY HOUSE
THE WHOLE WEEKEND

We tried to visit Aunt Frannie, but she didn't open the door and she doesn't answer when you call.

I showed Noa the cupboard in the attic and we managed to open the box! We had to ease the lid up with a screwdriver and the edge got a bit broken. I hope my mother doesn't notice.

Inside the box were photos of Ma almost naked, standing on the beach painting a picture. Another photo was of Matt in Madras's buttocks bobbing in the sea. There were also letters from him to Ma that Noa and I read out loud to each other. One letter said:

My sweetheart. This is my last letter to you. It's not your fault, it's mine. I have to spread my wings. I hope you can let me go free like the sea eagle I really am.

Matt had sent a picture of himself that my mother had drawn on with a felt pen.

"He broke her heart," said Noa.

We think that Ma got together with Dad before she'd got over Matt in Madras. That she is still unhappily in love with Matt. And that's why she sighs all the time.

We decided to help her. Now we have two jobs: get back Aunt Frannie's life-joy and get Ma to stop being unhappily in love with Matt in Madras.

I'd almost blocked out how much fun it is with Noa. We played with my stuffed toys and Noa joined the dots on my chicken pox scars. Then we pretended to have Tourette's and flapped our arms and said our ugliest words. When Noa's mother came to give Noa a ride home, I stood on the bed calling out: "Furuncle! Furuncle!"

CRICKET AND NOA'S UGLIEST WORDS:

DUDE
PRUNE
WIFE
PUBERTY
FURUNCLE
REGURGITATE
BROTH
JERKY
HONK
MOIST
MEATLOAF

26

Noa wasn't at school today and she's not answering her phone. What if she's changed her mind! Maybe she thinks I'm a baby, still playing with stuffed toys.

I had a stomachache the whole day. We made brownies in food tech and I got butter in my hair. Tomorrow we can take it home. The question is how much will be left because the food tech teacher usually sneak-eats our baking. She's very, very fat. Her last name is Cutter but everyone calls her Butter. Even Rock said it once. My mother said she feels sorry for Butter who can't help eating all our baking.

I got a note from Mitten to say he doesn't want to be with me anymore. So that problem is out of the way.

I ate lunch on my own. It was meatballs.

Aunt Frannie didn't open the door even though I know she's at home. I heard my parents talking earlier today. Dad was really worried and thought they should get Aunt Frannie back into the psych ward. Ma sighed and said she agreed. But I know that's the WORST thing they could do! Aunt Frannie will never get the joy of life back again at the psych ward.

Argh, I wish I could talk to Noa! But she seems to have been swallowed up by the ground. My potato heart is shaking. Don't know if I dare go to school tomorrow.

27

Noa is back in school! I'd just been to the food tech room
to get my brownie when I saw her. Sitting by the cupboard
with the horse girls and laughing. My potato heart sank
like a stone. The horse girls caught sight of me and
called out:

"Here comes Crapula!"

Noa looked at me for what felt like forever. As if the
seconds were made of tough, old chewing gum. Then she
jumped down, and I thought she was leaving.

She came straight over to me. And she smiled so all her
teeth showed.

"Hi, Cricket!"

We hugged. It really is us again!!!!

C † N

BF's to the end of space remote where god is a goat

Before long we were surrounded by horse girls: a fence of legs in white jeans.

"How can you hug her? She stinks of crap," they said.

"You're the ones who stink like crap. Horse crap," said Noa, and she took my hand, and we pushed through the leg-fence and ran. The horse girls galloped after us. At the end of the corridor, Noa pulled me into the bathrooms and locked the door. The horse girls kicked the door with their riding boots and neighed horribly.

Luckily, I had the brownie, so we didn't starve. And at first it was quite snug. We read the graffiti and made paper people and looked at clips of drum solos on my phone. (Noa's had broken—that's why we couldn't get hold of each other yesterday.) But after almost half an hour, Noa had had enough and asked for a felt pen.

I took my pencil case from my backpack and Noa chose a fat black marker. She wrote CRAPULA in big letters on her T-shirt. Then she wrote the same on mine.

"Now it's war." She pushed her finger into the icing on the brownie. She smeared it on her face. I did the same.

We looked at ourselves in the mirror and smiled so all our teeth showed. Then we stuffed our mouths full of brownie and opened the door.

"Wow, poop tastes great!" we yelled and opened our mouths wide.

One of the horse girls vomited into a bin.

I went to Aunt Frannie's with the last bit of brownie, but she didn't open the door today either, even though I called through the letter slot. I left the bag hanging on her door.

Noa rang. She's found Matt in Madras on Facebook! He apparently no longer lives in Madras, but in Mariestad, in Sweden. And he doesn't look at all like he did in the photos. It's as if his face was blown up like a balloon and then deflated. In one picture he's posing in an ugly cowboy hat outside a shopping mall. He seems to be with an old woman, or at least he's happily being kissed by an old woman with a chin that's melted over her throat.

When Ma came home I showed her the picture of Matt in Mariestad. She said nothing, but then she took out some ice cream even though it's a normal Stone Age Wednesday.

I was just about asleep when Noa rang again and said she
had a plan for how we could revive Aunt Frannie's joy
of life. She told me about a horse that she usually rides
called Sheriff.

"No one else wants to ride him because he hasn't got a
tail, just a little tuft that sticks out behind."

I didn't say that I'd spied on her and the horse girls and
knew exactly which horse she meant.

"I think it's time Sheriff came out for a moonlit ride,"
Noa said mysteriously.

29

The plan is that Noa will come and knock on my window
at three in the morning and we'll bike to the stables.
I'll hide clothes under my blanket so it looks like a body
and cut an end off my hair so it can stick out on the pillow.
IN CASE Ma and Dad look into my room in the night.
I think parents do that sometimes. Anyway, I saw a film
where two parents stood and stared at their sleeping child
and cried because they loved the child so much.

   At dinner, Dad and Ma looked like they were newly in
love. I almost dared hope for a little sister. My mother
normally notices when something is up and I'm really bad
at lying, so I said I needed to be by myself to grieve the
fact that I'm an only child. I'm so excited I probably won't
even fall sleep.

30

On the dot of three, there was a knock at my window. Noa was in the garden wearing pyjamas, a denim jacket and a ponytail. I fixed the bed, put a warm jacket over my nightie and climbed out the window.

We were quiet as we biked. The night was starry clear, and the full moon looked like a cheese wheel.

It was a bit creepy being alone at the stables and I worried we'd end up in prison when Noa found the key hidden under a bucket. We probably would be in prison if anyone had seen us. I don't think you can borrow a horse without permission, even for a good cause. But sometimes you have to do things you don't have permission for. That's what Rock told us. It's called *Civil Disobedience*.

It seemed as if Sheriff was waiting for us when we came to his box. He isn't much to look at but he has kind eyes.

Noa put a bridle on him and swung up onto his back. I had to use a bucket. Then we rode bareback through town, the whole way to Aunt Frannie's apartment.

We parked Sheriff outside her window and called her name, but the only person who woke up was an old man who shouted some ugly words. The main door was locked so we couldn't go up and call through the letter slot either.

"The old man'll phone the police," I said.

Noa looked disappointed. She clucked to get Sheriff to start walking but he refused and sort of shook his head. Suddenly he stretched out his white neck, snorted a few times and started to whinny. And what a WHINNY! It was so loud it echoed between the buildings, as if he understood that lives were at stake. That Aunt Frannie MUST wake up.

And she did! A light came on in her apartment, the window opened and she leaned out.

"You lunatics!" she yelled. "I'm coming down!"

Aunt Frannie had a red dressing gown on over her nightie. She stroked Sheriff on the muzzle and swung herself onto his back. Her hair was loose and she looked like a warrior princess in the moonlight.

We don't have a beach in our town, but Aunt Frannie thought the Swan Pond would be just as good. Noa and I sat in the grass. We could smell dogwoods and mud and suddenly it felt like summer. The night sky shimmered, the dew glistened and Aunt Frannie rode and rode. If a horse can look happy, Sheriff did. Aunt Frannie did too. Somewhere a trumpet played and Noa took my hand. The moon was reflected in the pond and it felt like all the stars in the universe were exploding in my chest.

Aunt Frannie rode so many laps around Swan Pond that she and Sheriff were both shiny with sweat.

"One last lap!" she called out, laughing.

Noa and I smiled so all our teeth showed and my potato heart did a flip.

When we'd said goodbye to Aunt Frannie and taken Sheriff back to the stables, we biked to the outdoor swimming pool to wash off the smell of horse, so our mothers wouldn't suspect anything.

We climbed over the fence, took off our clothes and held hands as we jumped into the pool. Then we floated on our backs and howled like wolves at the moon. It started to rain and all our clothes got wet, so Noa and I biked home in our underwear. We took our hands off the handlebars and it felt as if we were flying. We hugged goodnight under my window. Tomorrow after school we'll go to Aunt Frannie's and do art.

P.S. 1. This was the best night of my life.
P.S. 2. If I get a little sister, I'll call her Sheriff.

THE END.

This edition first published in 2022 by Gecko Press
PO Box 9335, Wellington 6141, New Zealand
info@geckopress.com

Distributed in the United States and Canada by
Lerner Publishing Group, lernerbooks.com
Distributed in the United Kingdom by
Bounce Sales and Marketing, bouncemarketing.co.uk
Distributed in Australia and New Zealand by
Walker Books Australia, walkerbooks.com.au

The cost of this translation was defrayed by a subsidy
from the Swedish Arts Council, gratefully acknowledged.

Gecko Press is committed to sustainable practice. We publish books to be read
 over and over. We use sewn bindings and high-quality production. Our new
books are all printed on FSC-certified paper from sustainably managed forests.

Edited by Penelope Todd
Typesetting by Katrina Duncan
Printed in China by Everbest Printing Co. Ltd,
an accredited ISO 14001 & FSC-certified printer

ISBN hardback: 978-1-77657-427-8
ISBN paperback: 978-1-77657-428-5
Ebook available

For more curiously good books, visit geckopress.com